Fireheart Tiger

ALSO BY ALIETTE DE BODARD

In the Vanishers' Palace
Of Wars, and Memories, and Starlight

DOMINION OF THE FALLEN
The House of Shattered Wings
The House of Binding Thorns
The House of Sundering Flames
Of Dragons, Feasts and Murders

THE UNIVERSE OF XUYA
On a Red Station, Drifting
The Citadel of Weeping Pearls
The Tea Master and the Detective
Seven of Infinities

OBSIDIAN AND BLOOD
Servant of the Underworld
Harbinger of the Storm
Master of the House of Darts

ALIETTE DE BODARD

FIREHEART TIGER

A TOM DOHERTY ASSOCIATES BOOK

NEW YORK

This is a work of fiction. All of the characters, organizations, and events portrayed in this novella are either products of the author's imagination or are used fictitiously.

FIREHEART TIGER

Cover art by Alyssa Winans
Cover design by Christine Foltzer

Edited by Jonathan Strahan

A Tordotcom Book
Published by Tom Doherty Associates
120 Broadway
New York, NY 10271

www.tor.com

Tor® is a registered trademark of
Macmillan Publishing Group, LLC.

ISBN 978-1-250-79327-0 (ebook)
ISBN 978-1-250-79326-3 (trade paperback)

First Edition: February 2021

Fireheart Tiger

They're coming.

It's early morning, the end of the Bi-Hour of the Cat—and Thanh has been awake for most of it, staring at the wall and trying to cobble together thoughts in the emptiness of her mind.

If she closes her eyes, she'll see Yosolis again, smell the snow and ashes on the night the palace burned—when everyone was too busy evacuating the real princesses to give much thought to the dark-skinned one in the attic room, the "guest" from the South who had been little more than a glorified hostage.

Thanh was sixteen then; she's eight years older now. It should mean eight years wiser, but instead she feels as hollow and as empty as she was at twelve, watching the shores of Ephteria loom into view for the first time, and thinking that alien and cold court would be her life, that the palace in the capital of Yosolis would be the gilded bars of her jail—and, worse, that Mother was the one who had made the choice for her, for the good of Bình Hải, her home country.

For her own good.

Thanh had returned to Bình Hải two years ago, a homecoming with fanfare and pomp that should have cemented her position near the apex of court. Instead . . . instead, she came back too soft, too pliant. Too thoughtful and discreet, Mother says.

A noise, as the door slides open. Ái Vân, her eldest handmaiden, her face carefully blank and composed. "Your Highness? It's time."

Thanh throws one last look at the papers on the bedside table. Reports from spies and magicians, assessments from advisers in the Ministry of Rites and the Ministry of War; everything chronicling the inexorable encroachment of Ephteria into their lives.

They're coming.

A trade delegation; a friendly visit from Ephterian delegates. They can all hear the words that aren't said, the truth of steel beneath the silver-tongued platitudes.

"I'm coming," Thanh says.

Ái Vân has the grace to believe her, to turn and wait for Thanh in the corridor when she composes herself.

Ancestors, watch over me.

As Thanh turns towards the door, something glimmers on the papers: something like a reflection of the sun, and then it stretches and grows, a long, slow trail of orange light like a finger trailing across the topmost sheet—for a moment only—and she holds her breath until it burns in her throat. Not today. She can't afford to have anything mysteriously catching fire in the bedroom. She can't have to explain to Ái Vân why things keep turning to cinders around her, as if the fire that burnt Yosolis and still haunts her nightmares had chosen to follow her home, burning ridiculously small things—orchids in vases, the hairs of calligraphy brushes, the vermillion ink of seals, small scraps of paper on her desk, pinches of tea leaves, badges of rank on five-panel dresses . . .

No no no.

The light sinks to the slow, lazy glow of embers: it's just sunlight coming through the closed shutters. Thanh exhales, and leaves the room—though she already knows that the fire will come back.

It always does.

~

In the throne room, Mother is waiting for her. She sits cross-legged on the dais, watching row upon row of assembled mandarins on either side of a richly woven carpet. In front of her is a simple low table with a teapot and three cups of tea. The familiar smell of the tea—cut grass and algae overlaying a sharp bitterness—prickles the back of Thanh's throat as she moves, bowing to Mother and joining her on the dais, kneeling in front of the teacups.

"Child," Mother says, inclining her head. "I hope you're ready."

Is she? Thanh tries to remember all she's read, the names of the major Ephterian traders, how many ships came and what they sold: what Ephterians value, what they want—everything she'd picked up in Yosolis without meaning to. "I don't know," she says, finally. Mother's glare stops her from elaborating. She knows what's at stake: Bình Hải's survival as a country. She knows, too, what Mother hopes: that her time in Ephteria helped her pick up insights and habits that will help build a rapport between the delegation and her.

But the only rapport Thanh built—the only insight she gained—is one of which Mother would not approve.

"They're here," Mother says.

Footsteps, from the small flight of stairs that lead up to the throne room. Shadows, crossing the threshold from the gardens into cool darkness. Mother's face is impassive.

They walk in three abreast, looking left and right at the sea of assembled officials and their square caps, at the carvings on the stone pillars, the dragons and the turtles fighting each other for swords and spears, the eunuchs bowing to them as they head up the dais, the lanterns hung in the rafters, the elaborate confections of carved wood and cloth dancing in the wind. They bow to Mother, but it is small and perfunctory. Thanh knows there was an entire negotiation involved in how deep that bow would be, that they utterly refused to prostrate themselves as any representative of a foreign state would, and that for a moment it looked as though Bình Hải would declare war on Ephteria then and there.

And behind them . . .

She walks tall and proud, unbowed, but her gaze is fixed straight ahead and doesn't waver. The sword at her side goes "tap, tap" against the rich weave of her trousers as her legs move. Thanh's hands itch, remembering how soft her skin was when she ran her fingers over her legs, when her lips grazed the pale skin of her neck, the same neck that's now hidden behind a high collar and a ruffle, the lips that are closed, the face bare of makeup, her fair skin glowing like white jade.

Eldris. Princess Eldris.

"Empress," Eldris says. She bows, a fraction longer, a fraction deeper, than her escort. Her eyes—her wide, blue eyes—rest on Thanh, and she smiles. "Princess. It is good to meet you again."

Eldris. Of all people, she wasn't expecting Eldris. Thanh remembers her—the same age, distant and un-attainable at first. She remembers the night of the fire, stumbling out of the burning palace with the serving girl

Giang suddenly falling behind her as the entire court turned to look—and, in the center of that press of dignitaries, Eldris's gaze resting on her, light and curious. Remembers the knock on her door a few months later, and the seventeen-year-old Eldris holding out a single rose to her with a crooked smile. There's nothing left to her but the frantic beating of her heart—all words scoured clean by fire, by memory. "Princess," she says, finally, and then stops. "You honor us with your presence."

"Oh, it's nothing. It does me good to see the business of statehood," Eldris says, her tone carefully neutral.

"So good to see you children remember each other," Mother says, but her gaze is sharp. Thanh has never told her much about her time in Yosolis, but what has Mother worked out anyway? "Come, Princess, have some tea." Mother pours, effortlessly, as Eldris sits: her overcurious attendants have settled behind her, glowering. "I trust your journey was eventless?"

Eldris shrugs. "The sea was restless. Sailors speak of angry dragon spirits. I'm glad that we were able to rest in Hồng Nam. Captain Pharanea"—she points to the eldest woman in the delegation—"fell badly sick on board and needed time to recuperate."

Captain Pharanea nods, gracefully. She looks unsettlingly pale, but the smile she flashes Thanh is pure predator. She is not in this delegation for show. "I'm all better now, Your Highnesses. And ready to get down to business." She opens her satchel, starts spreading papers on the table: an opening salvo done with as much care as the firing of weapons. "We have so much to talk about."

Thanh recognizes most of the papers Pharanea has put in front of her: letters from Ephterian merchants in their characteristic script, magistrates' official reports from Bình Hải, with the vermillion seals at the bottom, and maps drawn by Ephterian cartographers with the cardinal directions reversed compared to Bình Hải.

She slowly, deliberately sips her tea, trying not to look at Eldris—not to think of Eldris and the way that her heart still misses a beat whenever Eldris's gaze rests on her. The liquor is green and luminous and faintly tastes of the sea. "I'm so glad you're recovered." She hasn't brought her own papers from her room: she could have gone for the cheap and theatrical gesture, but she doesn't need to. "I see you've brought us trading disputes."

Pharanea bristles. "Disputes? I should think this is more serious." She opens her mouth, but Thanh gets there first.

"You're right." She's glanced at the seals, had time to sort out which magistrates they belong to. The province of Đại Ánh, and what looks like all echelons of the judicial hierarchy from county to prefecture. Time for a leap of faith. "Murder is always serious, isn't it? The deliberate snuffing out of a life. Depriving a child of their mother, parents of their filial daughter"—she knows that last won't carry as much weight with the Ephterians, who think filial piety rank superstition, but she has to say it, nevertheless—"an empress of her most dutiful subject."

Mother's face is set, unmoving. She doesn't speak. Letting Thanh take the lead, or simply waiting for her to make a mistake she'll get to berate her for?

A silence. Eldris says, softly, when Pharanea doesn't speak, "It *was* a trading dispute. A feud between merchants which led to Master Caeth and her clerks killing their Hải trading partner. We wouldn't want the Great Empress of Bình Hải to have to embroil herself in such petty things. Let us deal with the offenders. We can assure you they won't get off lightly."

Thanh inclines her head. The demand is clear. "Extraterritoriality," she says. Might as well bring things into the open. "You want Ephterian merchants to be exempt from local laws."

Pharanea starts, and looks at her a little more closely, as if an insect had suddenly learnt to speak. Thanh has to grant her that: she recovers quickly. "Of course not," she says. "We would never make such a demand of our valued allies. Merely in this matter—"

And in the next, and in the next: precedent in Ephteria has force of law. But they've brought up something else, too: the alliance. The guns and silver Ephteria sends Mother in exchange for the presence of the Ephterian merchants in Bình Hải; the vital link that enables her to maintain her throne, to send Thanh's elder sister Linh to quell rebellion after rebellion. It's not subtle, or unexpected. "As allies, we naturally would want to find the best solution for this," Thanh says. "We know that the Ephterian merchants have been grateful for the protection afforded by the Hải imperial escorts—"

Pharanea smiles, and it's all sharp, bone-white teeth. "Oh, they are most grateful. But we do feel we have been imposing. It would be easier, surely, if our merchants were able to defend themselves against the rebels."

So that's what they want. Not just extraterritoriality, but armies and positions.

"They are allowed guns already," Mother says, sharply—as Thanh watches, horrified, because she can't stop Mother from walking straight into the trap of this conversation.

"Oh, we weren't thinking guns, of course not. Our merchants are looking to defend themselves, not go on the offensive. No: it would be easier for everyone, wouldn't it, if they could make their houses stronger? If they could build thicker walls and better defenses—fortify against the rebels, and get a better quality of professionals manning these—"

Fortresses. Garrisons. Soldiers. That's what they want; what they've come here for. And they know—they've always known—that Bình Hải, propped up by Ephterian silver and guns and beleaguered by internal and external enemies, can't really afford to refuse them. "That may not be expedient," Thanh says, more abruptly than she's meant to, and she sees Mother's sharp inhale of breath.

"Is it not?" Pharanea smiles again. Eldris is still, carefully expressionless. "That's such a shame. I was under the impression the alliance had been mutually beneficial so far."

The threat isn't even subtle anymore. What do they have against it? A threat of their own, of seeking patronage from another northern country? A call to Ephteria's religious beliefs, beseeching them to have mercy on fellow souls? Thanh's gaze wanders around the room as she thinks—and that's when she catches, again, a glimmer of light. At first she thinks it's from the lanterns in the rafters—the embers burning in the daytime—but then she blinks again and it's at the bottom of her teacup, in the bunched and soggy tea leaves, slowly lengthening and stretching.

No no no.

Thanh draws in a deep, shaky breath—and before it has time to reach her lungs the leaves catch fire.

It's warm and orange: the color of the setting sun, of

the flames of the burning palace; she remembers the air smelling faintly of charred wood and molten stone. Small and insignificant, and Mother has gotten up and is arguing with Pharanea, a conversation Thanh catches only hints of because she's sixteen again, and running through the palace, holding the hand of Giang, the Hải serving girl she found shivering in the attic next to her own bedroom, and they're running and running, and the fire is in every room and in every courtyard, driving them again and again until it seems their only choice is diving through the flames, until all Thanh can think of is that burning will at least set them free—will at least allow her and Giang to finally breathe . . .

"Your Highness? Your Highness!"

When she opens her eyes again, they're all staring at her. She's set the teacup down. The leaves have stopped burning: the cup is filled with warm ash and the smell of the fire is spreading, filling her lungs and her mouth until everything tastes sharp and bitter. "I have to go," she says, forcing herself to speak through burning pain. "We can resume this conversation later."

And, slowly, deliberately, Thanh walks through the sea of assembled officials—waiting until no one can see her face anymore before she allows herself to finally relax.

~

Outside, on the stairs of the throne room, Thanh bites her lips until blood flows, but the taste of blood isn't sharp enough to wash away the ashes in her mouth. Below her, in the courtyard, Hải soldiers are exercising over the national insignia, the dragon wrapped around the pearl of the sea. The noise of their boots distantly drifts up to her.

It burnt. The tea burnt. Soggy tea leaves caught fire right in the throne room, in full view of everyone else. Not just in her nightmares or in her bedroom.

It's getting worse and her handmaidens won't be able to cover for her if it continues. Not in front of foreigners. What should she do? What can she do?

She can call in a priest—or a monk-exorcist. But if she does—if she does it now—the Ephterians will hear about it.

Worse, Mother will hear about it. Thanh is already such a disappointment in Mother's life: the princess sent away who came back, not brash and confident, but quiet and thoughtful. The princess who's not Linh with her martial prowess, or Hoàng, always ready with political advice. Thanh is only in charge of the negotiations because there's no better person, because Mother still has hopes that something can be salvaged of Thanh's childhood. To hear that Thanh has done nothing but bring nightmares and a curse of fire home ... No, she can't afford to have that happen or she will be sent in disgrace to the eastern provinces, given some plum but hollow appointment to save face.

She can do this. She can prove herself worthy. She can counter the Ephterian narratives so Bình Hải will survive. She can—

"Thanh!"

It's a voice she would know anywhere, one that reaches deep down into her belly and tightens a fist of ice around it. Princess Eldris has followed her onto the terraced area in front of the throne room. "Thanh!" she calls again.

What is she doing here? "Princess."

"Oh come, don't be so formal. Have you forgotten me already?"

Of all the things . . . Thanh takes a sharp, burning breath. "No," she says, finally—voices the fear she hasn't dared to give voice to. "I thought *you* had."

Eldris, after all, is the kind of princess who gets rescued. Who doesn't *need* to be rescued. The kind of princess who will become queen. And the kind of princess who, after the fire—months after she saw Thanh and Giang come out through those burning doors, months after they moved into a smaller palace in the city—turned up at the door of Thanh's bedroom with a single rose, wordlessly holding it out to her and smiling, the sparkle in her eyes suddenly making Thanh painfully aware of the emptiness in her chest.

"Oh, Thanh." Eldris smiles, throwing her head back in that achingly familiar way of hers. "Are you all right?"

Thanh's blood runs cold. "What do you mean?"

"You walked out rather abruptly. I understand Pharanea can be a bit unpleasant when she gets going, but I assure you she's not here as part of the war faction." Bitter laughter. "They were hard to keep from this delegation."

"War faction." Thanh keeps her voice flat. "Let me guess. People who just think Ephteria should take what it wants."

Eldris says, "We can't afford to conquer Bình Hải."

Yet. Thanh bites down on the word. Eldris goes on, "And we have no interest in doing so, in any case. Our merchants need customers to sell to, not terrorized or dead people." She almost said "natives"—Thanh can hear it in her voice—but she forced herself to stop in time. A visible effort, made for Thanh's sake. A peace offering. And she did ask. She could so easily have ignored Thanh's mood.

"I'm all right," Thanh says. "I just needed some air to think on what Pharanea said."

"Ah." Eldris smiles. She doesn't believe Thanh, but the lie wasn't meant to be believed. It was just social grease, intended to keep wheels turning. "Walk with me awhile, will you?"

Thanh looks back at the throne room.

Eldris shakes her head. "They're going over documents. Pharanea isn't going to bring anything new to the table."

Thanh says, slowly and cautiously, "You could just be trying to trick me."

Eldris's gaze rests on her, blue and unreadable. "Yes. But why would I leave the room if my advisers were going to do anything significant?"

"Mother—"

Eldris laughs. "She's faced down the Quỳnh and the Ngân Kỳ. Do you really think she needs a chaperone?"

She does, sometimes. She doesn't know everything. The thought is an unsettling stone in Thanh's belly. But Eldris's blue gaze draws her: the curve of her lips, the bare skin at the nape of her neck, the thought of running her hand over soft, translucent, yielding skin. "Let's go," Thanh says.

They walk along the edge of the raised platform, by the side of the pillars. Thanh doesn't know what to say: heart too large in chest, acutely aware of how everything about her feels sad and washed out. Eldris—who was never one for contemplative silence—breaks it without a trace of shame or regret. "How have you been?"

Thanh thinks of fire in her bedroom, of the long, long nights remembering what it felt like to be left to burn in the palace in Yosolis. She's so desperately lonely, in what should be her home. Sometimes she wishes Giang had come back with her. Thanh hadn't known Giang, not exactly—they only met the night of the fire, running through burning corridors—but she'd have had someone with her who understood. But Giang smiled at her and squeezed her hand, and disappeared into the crowd the moment the royal family came for Thanh. Not altogether surprising: What servant girl wants to be noticed by her masters? Fame is a double-edged sword. "I've been all right, I suppose. Busy."

Eldris laughs. "I can see. Good. It's high time she finally recognized that you're of age."

And no longer young enough to be a hostage, Thanh supposes. Two years home, a princess in her own right, with responsibilities of her own. She shouldn't be so resentful: it's unfilial and improper and she knows Mother had no choice if she wanted Ephterian support to maintain her throne against the usurper dynasty and the hunger of neighboring countries. She knows that Ephteria—of which Eldris is part—didn't give Mother a choice. Yet still . . . still, she feels like she's twelve again, watching the shores of Bình Hải recede, Mother standing expressionless on the quay, eyes shining with the reflection of the lanterns, watching her go and making no move to stop it, barely showing any sorrow or any other emotion. "How have you been?" she asks Eldris.

An expansive shrug. "Busy. The palace is still being rebuilt, but it'll take years, so in the meantime Mother has taken over Countess Sosheria's Winter Palace." She grimaces. "It's cramped and there's so little privacy I want to scream sometimes."

"I know the feeling," Thanh says, awkwardly. They're in the gardens behind the throne room now—a series of courtyards with flowers and ponds and carefully cultivated miniature landscapes from mountains to river shores. "It's the same here."

"Is it?" Eldris's voice is sharp. She looks around, a hand on her sword, casual and without a change of expression, but Thanh is sure that she's marking people, the guards behind the longevity walls, the ones monitoring the small solitary pavilions by lotus ponds. They've left behind their escorts and Thanh's handmaidens, but solitude is nothing but a carefully maintained facade. "Nothing changes, does it." She laughs, and it's utterly without joy.

Thanh's heart misses a beat. "You weren't so cynical."

"I suppose not," Eldris says. She looks at Thanh, cocking her head. "And you weren't this staidly formal. Is something the matter?"

Thanh thinks of Mother; of their beleaguered kingdom and negotiations from a position of absolute inferiority; of fire in teacups and in her rooms, always laying low and waiting to take from her. She thinks of Eldris, who's now sitting on the opposite side of a negotiation table and with whom she shouldn't be fraternizing. "You know," she says. "How everything has changed."

"Ah." They walk through courtyard after courtyard, going deeper into the garden. She stops at last, leaning against one of the pillars of a small pavilion, watching the pond: this one has an artificial island imitating a mountain, with a miniature temple clinging to its summit. Eldris looks around her, and finally shrugs, as if it's all out of her hands. "Thanh. Do you know why I'm here?"

"The Grand Tour," Thanh says, without thinking. Once, the Ephterians sent their golden youth to southern countries—to find sun-drenched ruins and dark-skinned, exotic locals to breathlessly write home about. Now the world has shrunk, and the far South—Bình Hải, Ngân Kỳ, and their neighbors—is the only adventure that will sate the depth of their thirst.

"That's what I need to do." Eldris laughs, sharply. "A chance to grow into the ruler of the country, for my advisers to meet your mother and bring their grievances to her." The hand on her sword has clenched, white-knuckled, over the hilt. "It's so nice to hide motivation in plain sight."

"I don't understand."

A sharp, wounding look from Eldris. "No, you don't, do you? Thanh, you're the reason I came here."

The reason.

Everything freezes. Thanh's heartbeat rising and rising, a panic in her throat, everything sharpening and narrowing to Eldris's face and Eldris's hands, now gently cupping her face—barely a pause to see if Thanh flinches, and then Eldris's lips are on hers, a cold shock that travels all the way into her chest. Thanh gasps, coming up for air. "You cannot possibly—" she starts, and has to stop, because Eldris kisses her again.

She tastes like snow—sharp and bracing, the cold giving way to a stinging sensation at the back of Thanh's throat—and Thanh is back, abruptly, in her bed in Yosolis, in the Winter Palace, Eldris's hands gently peeling off her dress and her undershirt, sliding it off her shoulders and then coming back to her shoulders and down again, stroking Thanh's skin again and again as if she could slide that off, too. Until desire rose warm and unbearable, as it is rising now, a warmth in her chest and between her legs that constricts all thought. "Eldris—"

"Sssh," Eldris says. She lays a finger on Thanh's lips, stilling them. Her smile is wide and infectious. "I've gone hungry for far too long, Thanh. And so have you. Haven't you?"

Something comes undone, then, within Thanh—a tight knot loosening at last, bonds slashed through, air into compressed lungs. She smiles, surprised to feel it doesn't hurt, and draws Eldris to her, feeling the weight of her on her arms, the reassuring solid presence—and every thought and worry melts into nothingness.

~

Later—much, much later—they lie tangled in the gardens, on the hard surface of a pavilion. Eldris brushes branches from Thanh's undone hair. "My sweet princess," she whispers. "I've missed you so much."

Thanh doesn't want to move. Moving means facing Mother, means going back to the negotiations and thinking of the best path forward. Moving means facing the fire and what it's doing to her life. "Do you ever think of the fire?" she asks.

Eldris stares at Thanh for a while, her hand still woven in the dark mass of Thanh's hair. "The palace one? No. I can't afford to spend my life afraid."

Afraid. Thanh tastes the word in her mouth, snow and ashes and bitterness. "You think it would happen again."

A shrug, from Eldris. "Fire is always with us. It keeps us warm in winter. And the pipes clog badly, regardless of what we do. Although"—she frowns, thoughtful—"that one didn't start in the walls or the hearth. According to Mother, it started in her library—in those little glass cases with the curio collections."

"The curios," Thanh says. She remembers in their headlong flight entering that room Giang falling to her knees in front of the glass cases, screaming she'd come from there. In Thanh's dreams Giang always catches fire, but in real life Thanh pulled her up—gasping at the unexpectedness of warm weight on her arms—and dragged her out into another courtyard and then into the gardens.

Something in the memory, though, just doesn't sit right, like a faint pain in a tooth, something she can taste at the back of her mouth. "Eldris," she says. "Do you remember that servant girl I asked you to search for?"

An arched eyebrow. "Vaguely? I recall it was not a productive search." They never found her. Eldris with the full might of the royal agents scoured the city, and no one ever came up with that name or with that description. Eldris frowns. "It was odd, actually, come to think of it. No one remembered a Hải girl employed anywhere in the palace at the time."

"I remember," Thanh said. "We fought over it."

Eldris grimaces. "Yes." She'd asked Thanh if she was sure of what she'd seen, in a tone that suggested she thought Thanh had hallucinated the whole thing. She couldn't grasp, either, why a serving girl was worth pay-ing attention to, at all. "That's behind us."

Is it? Thanh wants to say it, but she's afraid it'll break the moment. Eldris never liked being contradicted. She always got so frightfully angry when that happened. And she's right in one thing: it's weird that the earth seems to have swallowed Giang utterly—that she appeared and was gone without so much as a trace—and weirder still that Thanh keeps being so bothered by it years after the fact.

Where did Giang come from?

Again, that unease, as if Thanh were standing at the edge of a chasm and peering inside.

Eldris's hand rests, lightly, on Thanh's cheek, a touch of shivering warmth that makes Thanh ache to kiss her. "Anyway, the fire doesn't matter. There will be other fires, my love, and we will survive them all."

My love. She can't—no, she did say that and Thanh isn't imagining it at all, and is it different from their sleeping together? "My love," she says, tasting the words like an unfamiliar delicacy.

"You disagree?"

"No," Thanh says, hurriedly, braced for Eldris's anger. "Of course I don't—" She wants to say, *Of course I love you,* but it's too much, too fraught, and the only thing that comes out is the words that came out back in Yosolis, when she ended their casual affair before Eldris could

28

grow bored. "We can't do this." Even more so now, when Eldris is here—as what? As an ally who could turn enemy on a whim? As an antagonist in the negotiations that Thanh is leading?

"Can't do this? I'd say we have." Eldris leans on one elbow, watching her fondly—and under her gaze Thanh feels herself melting again, suddenly larger and more confident, seen and valued.

"You know what I mean."

"I know what you meant, back then." A frown. "But *you* know what you feel, Thanh."

She doesn't. It's all huge and fearful and out of control. "Eldris . . ."

"You love me. Don't you?"

Thanh hesitates, but doesn't it ring true? Isn't Eldris the more perceptive of the two of them? "It feels a lot like love," she says, and sees Eldris's smile.

"Good. Then that's all we really need to be happy, isn't it? Life is too short to be ringed by other people's expectations of proper behavior."

"You're a princess of Ephteria. The heir to the throne. You—" *You have better things to do with your time than bed a barbarian*—for that is all Thanh will ever be to the court of Yosolis, a curiosity, a savage from a land of huts and scattered villages. Thanh has better things to do than to consort with her opposite number when she should be rescuing them from the greed of Ephterian merchants.

"Ssh." Eldris lays a finger on Thanh's lips, stilling them again. "You worry too much."

Words press themselves behind Thanh's lips, but Eldris still holds them closed. She runs her finger on them, gently and insistently. Thanh stifles a moan. She finally manages to grab Eldris's hand before Eldris can slide a finger into her mouth. "Mother—" she says.

"What your mother doesn't know can't hurt her."

"So we're having a hidden affair?" The word feels alien and almost wrong.

"You want to call it something else?" Eldris's face is grave.

"I don't know what to call this at all," Thanh says, with stark honesty.

"Fair. Then consider: I don't know what to call it, either, but it's not a fling to me. This"—she lifts Thanh's hand up to her own lips, kisses it slowly for a stretched moment that Thanh wishes would never end—"this is utterly serious. Think on it, will you?"

~

Thanh wakes up gasping from a dream of Yosolis, feeling an unfamiliar, uncomfortable warmth.

The fire is on her hands, licking at a fragment of Eldris's hair that must have got caught beneath her nails.

No no no no.

She opens her mouth to scream, and it flickers out, leaving a faint warmth on her skin. She screams anyway, before she can think. "Leave me alone! What do you want from me?"

A silence. For a moment she feels absurd and alone, but then something glints, on the wood of her bed.

It's a patch of light like the reflection of a new year's lantern, and then it grows, little by little, expanding as it does—a fire in the hearth, the crackle of wood and the smell of burning filling the room—and then it's the shape of someone huddled on her bed, and Thanh's heart stutters and stops in her chest.

Who? What?

It's Giang, the serving girl. The one she was with when they escaped the fire at the palace.

How—?

She's disheveled, dark with soot and ashes, her feet bleeding, as if she'd been running with no shoes ever since that night so long ago.

"Giang?" Thanh reaches out before she can think, and then the Giang-shaped creature looks up, and her eyes are white and luminous, and her skin translucent like celadon, a thin layer of brown over the shape of fire.

"You're not her," Thanh says. A fist of ice tightens

around her heart, squeezes it into unbearable pain. "You can't just take her shape. You can't—please stop—" Words won't come—there's just a sharp, nauseous heaving squeezing the breath out of her, over and over again, emptying her mind of everything—not the fire, not the nightmares—she can't bear this anymore. "Please. Just leave me alone—"

Warmth on her, fleeting. When she looks up through eyes blurred with crying, the fire is still wearing Giang's shape, and holding something on her finger: a single tear, which she looks at as if it were a puzzle. It's already evaporating. "You don't remember me," she says. She sounds confused. "In the attic." And, when Thanh still doesn't speak, "In the cabinet room. I held your hand when we came out of the palace."

Thanh's blood freezes. Taking Giang's shape is one thing. Knowing their history . . . "You—" she starts, and then stops, because the words catch in her throat like barbed quills.

Eldris's voice says, in Thanh's memory: *It was odd, actually, come to think of it. No one remembered a Hái girl employed anywhere in the palace at the time.*

"I don't understand," Thanh says.

Giang hasn't moved. She's looking at Thanh with an odd hunger. "I am the fire," she says. "The one in the cabinets."

"You—" Thanh starts, stops again—and then flings herself, bodily, into the abyss. "You burnt the palace? You killed—"

"It was an accident!" Giang's face twists and flames flare beneath her skin. "I didn't mean to—" She takes in a deep, shaking breath, her eyes turning the white-orange of molten metal, quiets again. "They locked me in," she says, finally. "Took me from the temple and brought me to the palace. They put me on display." She opens her hand and on it is a small amber pendant in the shape of a tiger—a curio Thanh remembers from the cabinet, an old and rough Hải carving. A trader must have brought it to Eldris's mother, never guessing the glint of fire in its heart was a living elemental, or that the temple's spells had kept it safely imprisoned.

"On display."

"You know what it means," Giang says, and Thanh's heart twists in her chest, because she does. Because she remembers being trotted out in elegant dresses: a well-behaved, elegant child, the one the patrons would coo over, the little savage from the South being brought to civilization, saved from the barbarism of her own people.

"I didn't burn the palace!"

Giang's laughter is bitter. "I didn't mean to." She closes her eyes and the light in the room dims. "One of the serving girls opened the cabinet and touched the carving.

I could move. I could jump. I could escape"—she hugs herself, desolately—"except I didn't know where to. Except all the corridors looked alike and people screamed, and there was smoke and fire everywhere . . ." Her voice trails off. "I didn't know where to go. I didn't mean to." A pause. "I didn't remember that everything I touched caught fire."

Thanh thinks of the orchids falling to ashes. "You didn't disappear in the crowd. You've been hiding. In this room?"

Giang grimaces. "First in Yosolis, and then here. In this room. I followed you when you left."

"You followed me?" Thanh's breath catches in her throat. "You. You've been burning all those things around me."

"I didn't know where to go." Giang's grin is sheepish, but her gaze is desolate. "I have to burn," she says. "I have to feed. But it doesn't have to be that bright. It doesn't have to be . . ." She pauses, again, as if words were hard to get. "It doesn't have to harm."

It doesn't have to harm. Oh, ancestors. Thanh thinks of fire: thinks of what it must have meant to be contained within a small charm and then again within the confines of a cabinet, and then stretching at the taste of freedom, of running, endlessly lost within a nightmare of fire and smoke and not finding the escape she'd dreamt of. Thinking of what it must have meant, to burn only small and insignificant things for eight long years, to deliberately diminish herself the same way she'd been imprisoned in the carving. "You've been with me all that time." It's vertiginous and frightening, suddenly throwing the last eight years in a different light. "Watching me."

"No, I have not been spying on you. Your life was your own. I just needed . . . a safe place." Giang's smile is bright and carefree, and so achingly fragile. "You were kind to me that night in the palace. I thought you'd understand."

She's looking at Thanh with that expression on her face: trying to hide how much she's waiting on Thanh's approval, how much she's hoping—how much it'll hurt her if she doesn't get it.

Something shatters in Thanh's chest. She reaches out, grabbing Giang's hand before she can properly articulate what she's doing. There's that same weight she remembers, a reassuring firmness that spreads warmth into her limbs. "Oh, li'l sis," she says, the endearment coming instinctively to her. "Of course I understand." And, shivering, draws her nearer to her and hugs her until Giang's trembling subsides and she curls up in Thanh's embrace with a sigh that sets the lanterns in the rafters burning brighter.

~

Thanh goes to the ancestral halls.

She leaves Giang in her bedroom, sitting on the bed and curiously looking at everything from steamed buns to carving: the fire elemental keeps fluttering in and out of existence, first solid, then not, as if the slightest breath of wind could blow her away.

Thanh lights incense and prostrates herself in front of the altars of her foremothers—the empresses of the past, the archaic characters of their names giving way to modern script, and then to black-and-white portraits of women who look like they could take on the world, carrying swords as though they were extensions of themselves. "What do I do?" she asks.

She waits.

There's no answer but the gentle smoke of incense as it burns. What should Thanh make of this, of all of this? Giang doesn't seem fussed, but neither did she sound likely to leave. Sooner or later someone will find her. Sooner or later there will be an exorcist, or a monk, or both. They'll say it's necessary. That it's for the good of everyone; that fire needs to be caged and contained—that Giang burnt down a palace already. They'll ignore the grief in Giang's eyes and the way she's made herself smaller and smaller over the years, seeking an impossible atonement for what she'd done.

"Please help me," Thanh says. She doesn't know if they

will. What would her warrior ancestors make of her, of the spare daughter sent abroad and come back with only a dim sense of what home means?

No answer. The pictures glint like fire, and in their light she sees Giang's haunted face.

She walks out of the ancestral halls and back to her room.

Giang is waiting for her, sitting on the bed. "Are you okay?" she asks. She's nibbling on a steamed bun from the breakfast basket the servants left in Thanh's room. Her hair shines like dappled sunlight.

"I don't know," Thanh says, finally. She should pretend, the way she's always done, but something about Giang is familiar and comforting and she finds she has nothing to offer but the truth. "It's complicated."

"Ah." Giang fishes in the bamboo basket, and holds out another bun. "Want one?"

Thanh can't help laughing. "Why not?"

They nibble together in companionable silence. Giang says, "Humans are weird. Why is there an egg yolk in the center?"

"You don't like it?"

Giang makes a face. "No, but—but how did you get the idea in the first place?"

"It's for wealth," Thanh says, and she wants to laugh again. All her problems suddenly seem very far away.

"Like coins at the hearts of buns."

Giang makes a face. "You can't eat coins."

"True. But you can eat salted egg yolk." Thanh thinks, for a while, on wealth and coin and commerce. She doesn't know what to do—about Giang, about Eldris, about any of what she's embroiled in. "I need to write letters." She holds up a hand to forestall Giang. "But you can stay here if you want."

Giang smiles. "There are more buns."

She's lying on the bed, taking the bun apart with the focus and attention of a very small child and making the occasional delighted noise. Thanh sits at her desk, writing with a brush—the sound of Giang's laughter soothes and delights her, keeps her bolstered as she does what she needs to.

She writes to the Quỳnh, to the Ngân Kỳ, to all of their neighbors. She tells them about the Ephterians, about the North, about the necessity of banding together to hold themselves together. Xứ Quỳnh Hoa is small and landlocked, but its warriors are fierce, and Ngân Kỳ . . . The Ngân Kỳ are Bình Hải's former masters, before the Hải declared their independence and made themselves a space of their own on the continent. They've had two centuries of freedom, but now Ngân Kỳ itself is weak, beset by internal wars, and the northerners are encroaching there, too. Thanh hesitates for a moment, and then writes of the sea becoming mulberry trees, of a time of trouble and upheaval, and offers Ngân Kỳ an alliance: mutual access to each other's markets, and help fighting off the northerners, in exchange for silver. Ngân Kỳ is poorer than Ephteria, but if Bình Hải taxes their merchants and if Bình Hải's merchants can sell their silk and pottery into Ngân Kỳ's much larger markets . . . then they can make it work.

The time for equivocation is past, and she'll need all the help they can muster if they are to survive.

A knock at the door. Giang startles. "I'll go." And she vanishes like a blown-out candle.

It's Ái Vân, an unreadable expression on her face. "Your Highness . . . you have a visitor."

Eldris? But why would she? Surely she, more than anyone else, knows that they have to keep their relationship a secret?

Thanh looks up and sees Captain Pharanea.

Ái Vân quickly and unobtrusively goes around the room picking up Thanh's letters and then exits, bowing to Captain Pharanea. She looks worried and why wouldn't she?

"This is irregular," Thanh says, after Pharanea has bowed to her. "We have official sessions and official channels."

Pharanea smiles, her eyes glinting like steel. "For official things, we do."

"I don't understand—"

"I know," Pharanea says.

"You what?"

A smile that is all unpleasant sharpness. "What you get around to in the pavilions of such widespread gardens."

Eldris. "We've done nothing," Thanh says. She feels chilled, and trapped.

"Oh, don't give me that." Pharanea walks into the room as if she owns it, pulling out one of the dragon-carved chairs and lounging in it. "I know why she came. She's hardly ever bothered with politics before, and certainly not with boring negotiations such as these." She scoffs. "Of course it had to be about something else. War, or a woman. Or both."

Thanh says nothing. She doesn't have any words left. "I don't understand. There's nothing wrong here. No mutual agreements."

"Oh, plenty wrong," Pharanea spits. "The wrong time and the wrong person. But then she's always had a wandering eye."

"She wouldn't—"

"Don't bother," Pharanea says. "She likes the unattainable. Challenges. And then she discards what she's got as she has so many broken toys. You're hardly her first."

Thanh   opens   her   mouth   to   say   Eldris

wouldn't—surely she meant it when she said it was serious—but then something deeper and colder, some gut reflex, stops her, and the negotiator in her takes over. "You're not here to insult me, I assume."

A snort, from Pharanea. Reluctant, grudging admiration. "No, I'm here to warn you."

"You've done it. Now what?" That's not what she's really here for: She's angry, and she wanted to sharpen her claws on Thanh. Make her as uncomfortable as possible, but it's not her end game.

Pharanea smiles, again. "I could require you to be removed from negotiations. Conflict of interest."

"You'll find that doesn't move Mother much," Thanh says. She keeps her face smooth and blank, but it costs her. Mother doesn't know and she cannot know. She won't stand for it: for the betrayal of Thanh sleeping with their overbearing, controlling partner that always seems on the verge of becoming their conqueror. For her making Bình Hải vulnerable because she can't do as simple a thing as controlling her lust.

"Oh, won't it? But I forget—your mother doesn't know."

Thanh opens her mouth to say *don't,* closes it—but it's already too late.

"So *that* you do care about." Pharanea shrugs.

"What do you want?"

"Oh, such unseemly haste. Did you not learn patience in Yosolis?"

Thanh has had enough of games. "What I learnt in Yosolis is that even the oldest stone can burn."

Pharanea grimaces. "You posture, but it won't avail you of anything, Princess. What do I want? What everyone would want, in my situation."

A favor. Thanh's weight brought to bear in the negotiation—and isn't that a formidable asset to have, the chief negotiator of Bình Hải secretly on her side? "You'll have to be more specific."

A smile. "You'll find that I don't have to."

So, not just a favor. An unspecified, untimed favor. A blank bank draft. "That's too much."

"Do you want me to take this up with your mother, then?"

"No." Thanh thinks of Mother—quick to anger, quick to discard the flawed, the weak. "Don't."

"Good." Pharanea smiles. "I didn't think she was right to pick someone so uncouth, but perhaps you *are* capable of learning proper manners. So good to see we're seeing things from the same point of view, Princess." She gets up from the chair, pushes it so that it scrapes on the floor, the wooden parquet screaming under the weight of its legs. "We're going to have such a lovely time together."

~

Thanh takes a deep, shaky breath. In her clenched hand is the summons to Mother's chambers. A simple message with her seal, brought by Adviser Long, one of the eunuchs who has been with Mother the longest.

The Empress of Heaven, the Fateful Prosperity Ruler, summons Five-Pearl Princess Đoan Thanh to an audience.

It's in the script of the court and below Thanh's full name it also lists each of her titles—not that the list is long—and it includes things like "The Princess Who Went to the Heart of Winter," as if being sent to Yosolis as a child is some kind of achievement worthy of being endlessly recorded and celebrated.

There's only one kind of formal summons that warrants Adviser Long: a reprimand.

Mother knows. Thanh doubts Pharanea told her—and she's only seen Eldris on the other side of the table in official audiences, but it's been so hard to keep impassive and casual, and of course Mother would see it. Of course.

She's not twelve anymore. She's the woman Eldris came all this way for—the woman with whom things are utterly serious. She is . . . desired. She can bear her mother's displeasure. She—

Everything she has—every appointment, every

title—flows at the empress's pleasure. She's Thanh's living ancestor and her elder, and she's owed not only respect but also filial piety, that of a subject for her empress, and that of a daughter for her mother.

It will be bad and there's nothing she can do about it.

And Giang hasn't been back. She vanished when Pharanea came in and hasn't returned. Thanh could use her now: could use the easy, relaxed companionship they seemed to have when she was writing letters—but who knows what drives a fire elemental? No, there is no hope here: it's just Thanh and the summons, and whatever may come of it.

She crumples the summons and—taking a deep, burning breath—enters the room.

Inside it's dark and cool and smells faintly of incense. Mother sits on a dais in front of a chessboard that's been cleared of everything save a couple papers. Her golden crown, flaring on either side of her, frames her face like the wings of a bird of prey, and her lips are tight with displeasure. Thanh doesn't even need to be close to feel the tension in the air. "Child," Mother says. It's short and snappish.

Thanh comes closer, and bows, head touching the floor. "Mother. I humbly apologize, but—"

Something hits her: the papers, thrown at her face. "How dare you, child? How dare you offer what is not yours to offer?"

Thanh pulls herself up, pushing the papers aside. "Mother, surely I—" And then she stops, because she's seen the script on the papers. It's not Ephterian. It's a forceful character, not in alphabet, but in the Ngân Kỳ language. It's a letter and it's addressed to her, but she's never seen this before. It has to be an answer to the letters she sent before Pharanea came to her chambers.

Of course. Still on her knees, Thanh makes a show of putting the Ngân Kỳ letter aside, but she uses that time to quickly scan it. Only a few words and sentences, but they tell her all she needs to know. All she needs to defend herself against. "I had to," she says.

"To bypass me and offer diplomatic ties to our old masters?" Mother's voice is cold. "I put you in charge of negotiations. I didn't give you license to bow and scrape to those who already conquered us once."

"I offered an alliance." Thanh keeps her voice low and even. She pulls herself up, then—watching Long. The eunuch's face is closed, but he's frowning. Not entirely in agreement with Mother, then. "As with any alliance, the final word on the terms would be yours. And the final rejection, if you wanted."

"I didn't give you leave."

"We need options!" Thanh says, finally throwing filial piety, and caution, to the winds. "We can't just keep depending on Ephteria to maintain ourselves! We can't negotiate from a position of utter dependence." She stops. It doesn't matter. None of it matters, because Pharanea is going to make sure it doesn't. Thanh won't be able to say no to whatever terms the Ephterians offer, because her secret still holds, because Mother doesn't know about her and Eldris—and she ought to be feel relieved, but all she feels is a sickness in her belly, as if someone were slowly slicing through her innards with a blade. She's burnt her bridges asking Ngân Kỳ for an alliance, and it'll be for nothing.

Long says, "Your Highness."

Mother's face is cold. "You'll defend her?"

"Princess Thanh merely did what she thought was best," Long says, slowly and smoothly. "As you taught her from the earliest age."

Thanh has a flash of herself at twelve again, watching the shores of Bình Hải recede, watching Mother's face, which is expressionless. Not a tear, not a frown, as if it cost her nothing to send a daughter abroad. But of course Thanh had been nothing more to her than a bargaining chip—her worth measured by her usefulness, by how much Mother gained from Thanh's presence in Yosolis. Silver and guns, and look what this bargain has wrought. Look what position it's left them in—Thanh has hollowed herself, and doesn't even have any value to show for it.

"A dutiful daughter," Mother says.

Long's voice is soothing. "Always."

A pause. Then Mother says, to Thanh, "No letters to other countries."

Thanh opens her mouth, closes it. "I can't negotiate if you tie one hand behind my back!"

"Then maybe you shouldn't be negotiating at all."

It would be so much easier, wouldn't it? Pharanea would ask for her favor, but Thanh wouldn't be in a position to grant her much of anything. She could go on with Eldris, could work out what to do with Giang—except she'd once more be small and insignificant, and at the mercy of what others choose to do to her. "No," she says. "Please give me another chance." And, slowly and carefully, forcing herself to sound quiet and humble when she feels anything but, "A scholar is nothing without the four jewels in their study." Meaning that no one can write without paper or brush or ink, or inking stone, and neither can she negotiate without leverage.

A silence. Long isn't speaking, and Thanh is kneeling, unable to see Mother's face. Finally Mother says, "I will do anything, use any means, to ensure that Bình Hải survives. Do you understand?"

Of course she does. Of course she always has. Everything and anything will be sacrificed on that altar. Mother will use any means, and any people. She's been doing it too long to see how much it twists everything around her. "I know this. Let me do the same." She has to try. Even if Pharanea hobbles her, even if negotiations are fraught and complicated by that favor she can't get out of owing, there has to be something she can do. Ephteria needs trade and the money from the trade, too: there must be something she can exploit there.

A snort, from Mother. "Fine. You will run your letters through Long before sending them."

Thanh lets out a breath she wasn't aware of holding. "Thank you, Mother."

"Don't thank me. Get out, and get us a bargain that will keep us alive and fighting."

~

Thanh gets out and into the gardens—to the pavilion where she and Eldris made love—with the letter from Ngân Kỳ in her lap, the only thing she's been allowed to keep after her audience. She reads it, slowly and carefully—and then stares at the sky, blinking back tears.

There's no salvation there. Ngân Kỳ is skittish: they're unhappy at the current state of things, but not near unhappy enough.

It is true that the foreigners have been acting like barbarian louts, not understanding propriety or benevolence or righteousness, but they have brought much into the country . . . It is, after all, our duty to be an example to children, and likewise our behavior will be a model for them. In time, they will learn to become filial . . .

Thanh thinks of Captain Pharanea and of Eldris—Eldris, who loves Thanh but doesn't have respect for either Thanh's mother or her own. They won't learn. They're convinced of their own righteousness. They bring silver and guns and expect everything in return. But of course Ngân Kỳ won't see this until it's too late.

What would it take, to break free of their hold?

The thought chills her. For as long as she can remember, the Ephterian merchants have been around. There used to be priests, too, but Mother banned them after they financed a rebellion against her. But the merchants stayed: the silver and the guns they carried were too valuable to throw out. And where the merchants are the politicians follow.

Like Eldris.

She remembers Eldris's hands on her skin and the feeling of satiation after they made love—that feeling of being seen, of being valued for who she is and not for what she can be bargained for. She remembers how good it felt, like an awakening.

It's not Eldris who is the problem, but the problems have come with Eldris, and they can't be untangled anymore. Ephteria is here to stay, and Thanh's relationship with Eldris, and Pharanea's blackmail, and Mother's hostility to any other alternatives just make everything inextricably tangled, inextricably worse.

What she and Eldris have is an affair: the same thing she and Thanh had in Yosolis, the thing Thanh ended after six months because she knew Eldris would grow tired of her, the same way she grew tired of all her other lovers once the novelty faded. She can't ask Eldris for help, because Eldris won't stand up for her. Pharanea is right: she'd never stood up for any of her previous conquests, no matter her protestations of love. And . . . if she does ask Eldris to intervene and Eldris says no, what then?

She's scared. So deeply, deeply scared of what will happen, of what it all means.

It's like she walked into a trap with her eyes wide open and now she's struggling at the bottom of a dark pit with the sky impossibly high, impossibly out of reach. If only she could grow wings. If only she could walk away from it all and still earn Mother's regard, still have Eldris's . . . affection or desire or whatever it is that they have, the thing that she still can't name.

She misses Eldris so much.

She stares at the letter from Ngân Kỳ, her eyes catching again and again on the word "righteousness," and abruptly it's like some dam she's never known was there breaks and she's weeping in uncontrollable fits that wrack her whole body, heaving and heaving with the taste of salt in her mouth, and the sharpness of the tea she's drunk this morning before coming to Mother's audience—the unfairness of it all, the impossible tangle of the situation, the blackmail she can't get out of, the relationship with Eldris that might not even be worth any of this, that might be nothing more than a fling—

A sound overhead. A clink of metal on wood, as if something were swinging in the breeze. A smell she can't quite identify—and a warmth on her hand.

"Big sis."

It's Giang.

"I thought—" Thanh starts. Her mouth and nose feel clogged with salt water. "I thought you were gone."

Giang shrugs. She's translucent: a faint outline against the pillar, scattered gleams of firelight that barely suggest the shape of a woman. A thin thread of light ties her to one of the lanterns overhead, and the smell is burning wood, the last of the embers in the lantern consuming itself. "I left for a bit because I got scared. Too many people in your chambers. Too much noise." A wistful, haunted look that breaks Thanh's heart. "Humans are scary."

Thanh tries to laugh, but everything is clogged with

tears and snot. "That they are, yes. I'm sorry they frightened you."

A shrug, from Giang. "It's nothing. I'll recover." A pause, then, "Everything that burns in the palace calls to me, big sis. And you're upset."

"It's nothing." She can't ask Giang to step in, not when Giang is herself running scared.

"Is it?" Giang's voice is sharp. She's wearing men's clothes, a scholar's tunic, and her hair is now done in the elaborate topknot of officials, the sash around her chest the color of washed-out celadon.

Thanh says, finally, "I don't know what to do."

Giang is silent for a while. "I don't know what's wrong. Is it the woman who came to your chambers?"

"You heard that? I thought you'd already left."

"Not entirely." Giang's voice is hesitant. "I was . . . curious. But I couldn't follow what you were saying." She purses her lips. "Human diplomacy is so complicated. I just know she threatened you. I didn't think it was that serious."

Thanh hesitates. It's clear that Giang doesn't know anything, and clear, too, that she's not playing any of the games the likes of Pharanea so love. Her power is raw fire—burning and charring—but she wields nothing else. Not even control over herself.

Oh, li'l sis. She wants to hug Giang, suddenly, but feels

too ashamed and too self-conscious about it.

She could tell Giang the truth. She could admit it all—Giang might be a stranger, but she has no stakes here. She won't judge. She won't try to affect anything. Out of everyone around Thanh, she's most likely to sit and listen, the way a supportive friend would. But she can't say it out loud: the blackmail, her relationship with Eldris, everything she's been keeping quiet. She just can't take that risk. So instead she lies—smoothly, easily, with the same smile she brings to the negotiation table—"Pharanea tried to threaten me into doing her bidding and Mother found out."

Giang kneels by Thanh's side, her hand resting on the polished wooden floor, a hair's breadth away from her. She smells warm and comforting, which is absurd because Thanh barely knows her.

But, in a way, she feels like she's known Giang for a long, long time, ever since the night of the fire. "She was angry," Giang says, finally. "Your mother."

Thanh closes her eyes. She could lie further, but all that comes out is the bitter truth. "All I hear is her disapproval. She thinks I'm still a child. A bargaining chip who didn't turn out the right way. A clumsy oaf who can't be trusted to do the right thing."

"She'd dismiss you?" Giang's voice is quiet. "Remove you from the negotiations?"

Thanh closes her eyes. The insides of her eyelids feel wet with misery. "Oh, she already threatened that. And if she thought she'd gain any kind of advantage . . ." She laughs, bitterly. "She'd ship me off to Ngân Kỳ or Xứ Quỳnh Hoa tomorrow. I'm the spare. The one she doesn't really need. She's got Linh and Hoàng—my sisters—for everything that matters."

A silence. Then Giang's touch, a faint warmth on her cheeks—not the fire of her nightmares, not the smoke and choking air of the palace, but something trembling and vivid and breathless. "You matter."

Thanh lifts her gaze, then. Giang is in front of her, not limned by light so much as made of it, a sketch of a human being, with those huge, luminous eyes trained on her. "Li'l sis," Thanh says, and she's not sure what she's choking on.

Giang's hand moves, to rest on her lips.

"Li'l sis," Thanh says, again, and then Giang looks beyond her, startled; and vanishes into nothingness.

Thanh turns, and sees Eldris.

She's walking towards her with that same brash confidence, as if she owned the gardens and everything within. Thanh pulls herself up, forcing herself to breathe. She still feels Giang's warmth on her cheek, on her lips, and she doesn't know anymore what she's meant to think about Giang.

"Thanh," Eldris says. She grabs Thanh's shoulders, her sword in its scabbard swaying, bumping against Thanh's legs. And, when Thanh doesn't move, Eldris gently runs a hand through the sticky mess of Thanh's hair, untangling hair and silver pins that fall to the floor. "My love. What's wrong?"

Thanh finally says, "Mother." Words have scattered in her mind.

"About us?"

Thanh shakes her head. "No. About the negotiations."

"Ah. Yes. She thinks you're not doing your job properly." A gentle sigh. "Thanh, whatever you do, she'll never approve."

"No. She—"

Eldris shakes her head. "You're the thing she's shaped. The puppet she made. Of course she'd never expect you to be other than what she wants in every one of your acts. She didn't designate a head negotiator. She named her surrogate."

You will run your letters through Long before sending them. And, of course, Long will bring them straight to Mother, querying for her approval in the least details.

"I can't do miracles!" Thanh says, and she thinks of Pharanea, of blackmail, and of what will happen when Mother finds out about her and Eldris. "I can't—" She says it slowly, in a barely audible exhale. "I just can't do it at all."

"Oh, Thanh." Eldris gently pulls Thanh's arms apart, and then pulls her upright—but Thanh can't really, so she ends up leaning against one of the pillars of the pavilion, still shaking. "Of course you can."

"You—you're the opposite side! How are we supposed to do this at all, how are we supposed to keep this hidden? How are we supposed to see each other within the walls of a palace where every guard reports to my mother? How—"

"Thanh—"

"I told you. We can't do this. We shouldn't be doing this. It doesn't matter how much I want it, how much I need it. We need to stop."

Eldris's face is still, as white as snow on stone. "How much you want it."

Thanh kisses her—lips on lips, feeling the warmth of Eldris's face—slowly at first, and then her tongue finds Eldris's and she's desperately trying to breathe in all of her. "I love you."

"I love you, too." The words in Eldris's mouth are desperate and fast, as if she's been hungering to say them for far too long. "Come with me, Thanh. Come home."

"I told you. We can't—"

"Can't?" Eldris's voice is sharp, almost wounding. "Marry me, Thanh."

The word is like a gunshot. "You want me to—"

"Be my wife. Please. I'll ask your mother, and that will bring it all out in the open. But you're the one whose opinion matters. The only one."

Her wife. That's not possible. Thanh says the only words that come to mind. "That's too much."

"Too much? Oh, sweetheart." Eldris holds her face close to hers, so that Thanh is staring into sea-blue eyes. "Do you truly value yourself so little?"

She's always been . . . the younger child. The bargaining chip. The hostage. That someone, anyone, would see beyond that . . . "I don't know."

"Then let me know for you," Eldris says. "Come to Yosolis and be my consort." She kneels, then, holding Thanh's hand as if to kiss it. "Do me the honor of being my wife."

She wants to, so desperately. And yet . . . something warm and unexpected stirs within her, a remnant of fire as bright as Giang's. She thinks of Pharanea and the ugliness in her face when she spoke of Thanh's uncouthness, of the way she could be brought to learn proper manners. "Your advisers will see me only as a prize from a country you've conquered."

A silence. She's gone too far—she sees Eldris's face go white, sees the way her hand wraps itself around the hilt of her sword. "I'm sorry. I shouldn't—"

"Fuck my advisers," Eldris says. "They'll have to understand that my wife's home is untouchable."

Untouchable. Pharanea, rendered toothless and powerless. It feels like a fairy-tale wish, the barbed and dangerous kind. She should be happy. She should be elated. And yet . . . "Eldris."

"There are other countries," Eldris says. "Xứ Quỳnh Hoa. Ngân Kỳ. Other outlets for our merchants." She smiles, and it's all edged teeth, and Thanh feels queasy without knowing why. "They can look elsewhere. Bình Hải will be safe. I promise."

"Safe." The word tastes alien and wrong, like something she's never really known.

"Oh, Thanh. I'm sorry. I just cut you out from your own responsibilities, didn't I? The negotiations. Of course I don't want to leave you with nothing to do and no power. You can still be head negotiator. You can come with us to Ngân Kỳ and make them agree to our terms."

"Head negotiator." It all feels unreal. Like she's been handed everything she needs, everything she's ever wanted. Like a gift that will melt or grow barbs any moment.

Eldris still holds her hand. Thanh feels the warmth of her—sees herself reflected in Eldris's eyes, a tall and beautiful princess, someone worth loving, worth fighting for. Worth ten thousand kisses and more. "Will you be my wife, Thanh?"

"Yes," Thanh says—and, kneeling, kisses Eldris, hard and long, staring into her blue eyes until every little bit of disquiet, every objection and every fear, dissolves into a rush of happiness.

~

"So, how go the negotiations, child?" Mother moves her red elephant away from the river in the center of the chessboard to block Thanh's black soldier.

They are playing their weekly game of chess, the one occasion when Thanh is alone with Mother for a perfectly plausible reason, without having to ask for a specific audience. Eldris—always rash and ready to rush into any fight—wanted to publicly propose to Thanh in the middle of the negotiations to force Mother's hand. It took strenuous arguing from Thanh to change her mind, and even then she's not altogether sure it was the right thing to do. It's a better solution to ask privately—that *she* ask privately—but is it going to be enough to satisfy Mother?

She moves her black general back to the center of the palace, biting her lip. The board is a mess: Mother has lost pieces slowly and steadily, including one of her two advisers. Two of Thanh's soldiers have crossed the river, but they're hampered by Mother's cannon. How much can

Thanh admit to? "I bartered them down to one fortress instead of one in every trading post. We're currently arguing location." And Pharanea still hasn't said anything: What is she up to? Not that it matters: once this game is over Pharanea's hold on her will be a fraction of what it was. Not wholly gone: she'll have to tread carefully in this interview, or Mother will take the pre-proposal liaison as a personal affront.

"Mmmm. What do they want?"

"Mouth of the Red River."

"No," Mother says, moving her cannon over a soldier to take one of Thanh's chariots, which she lays by the side of the board. "That's one of our two accesses to the Eastern Sea. Too strategic. What else?"

Thanh bites her lip, again. She moves one of her elephants away from the river, leaving Mother a wide opening. "I thought the Jade Mountains. It's sparsely populated up there."

"With vital goods," Mother says, sharply.

Of course she'd never be happy. Thanh waits, in silence, for Mother to offer her solution: the only one she'll deem acceptable. "They can have Bạch Điện."

"It's ruins," Thanh says, shocked. The old Hương places, the ones conquered by Bình Hải an age ago—haunted by the ghosts of slaughtered princesses and dismembered priests.

"Which bring them quite a handy profit."

"Only because there's enough space there for them to build large warehouses, and because the Red River is friendly there."

"Precisely. Don't underestimate the value of an anchorage."

"I don't," Thanh says, frustrated. Her hand hovers over a cannon—she hesitates, and moves a soldier instead, across the river that separates the board in half. A tactically unsound move, but her goal isn't to win the game. "But anchorage isn't what Pharanea wants." Of course it's not. Of course they both know it: that the fortresses they're asking for aren't really to protect their traders. They want to make inroads into Bình Hải itself. They want to be in a position to put more pressure on the country, and it's Thanh's job to find a place that gives them that impression while actually giving them more power. "Jade Mountains gives them the impression they're getting a stranglehold on our agarwood trade, but we can actually buy some from the Quỳnh."

"We're at war with the Quỳnh." Mother's voice is mild, but it has the strength of a full-on reprimand. "Did you already forget that? With your elder sister on the front lines, too." She moves her remaining chariot behind of her cannon, presumably in preparation for the cannon to take one of Thanh's pieces.

Linh is on the front lines of everything—the princess Thanh will never be.

Not if she stays here, in Mother's stranglehold. She hears Eldris's voice in her mind. *Thanh, whatever you do, she'll never approve.* "Fine," she says, finally. "I'll offer them Bạch Điện."

"Mmm." Mother frowns at the board, and then up at Thanh. "Child?"

"Yes?"

"What are you up to?"

"I don't understand," Thanh says, heart madly beating in her chest. *She knows.* Of course she'd notice Thanh's odd behavior.

Mother's hand sweeps the board. "By this time of the game you've usually checkmated me twice or three times. And taken half my pieces. Instead, all you've been doing is moving the same pieces around the board, with a few added ones so I won't notice what you're doing."

"Mother—"

"I didn't get to be Empress of Bình Hải by having no brains. And no eyesight." Mother's voice is stern.

"I don't see what you mean." Thanh wasn't expecting to have this conversation for another few turns at least—let Mother checkmate her once, let her feel a warm glow of happiness that things are going her way both in the game and outside of it. But it's all going sideways.

"Out with it." It's an order, not a request, and there is no choice.

Thanh moves her general back to the center of the palace. Should she kneel? Something in her revolts at the thought. "I've said yes to a proposal."

"Proposal." Mother's voice is flat. "You're my daughter. I handle proposals. Who—" And then she stops, because there can only be one person involved. "One of the Ephterians. *Her*."

"We love each other." Thanh's voice is more defiant, more pathetic, than she'd like. "She wants me to be her consort. To take me with her on the rest of the Grand Tour."

She's braced for an explosion, but when she looks up Mother is staring at her with an odd expression on her face. She's playing with one of the game pieces: the adviser that Thanh took from her. She says, finally, "When I sent you to Yosolis, you were too young."

But old enough to be traded away for Ephterian support. Thanh clamps her lips on angry words, feels them bubble up, bitter and sharp, raw inside her mouth.

Mother goes on, "And then the fire . . . I'm glad you came back, but I know that it changed you. That"—she stares, for a while—"that you were too vulnerable and too influenceable, and Eldris—"

What— "You think that's what happened? That I was *groomed* to fall in love with her? That she took advantage of a *child*?" *Does she—does she have any idea what she's saying?* "Just because you don't like us doesn't mean we're unnatural!"

"Of course not." Mother's face is hard, angry. "You don't understand, do you?" And then, in a softer voice, "She's here to take what she wants. And she won't take no for an answer."

"And you think it's wrong."

A sigh. "No. I think you're my daughter and I'd like to see you safe."

"Safe?" It's too little, too late: false, edged protestations of love and concern. "You have no say in what's happening here," Thanh says, fighting back tears. This wasn't how the conversation was supposed to go. "I don't need to be protected anymore." She needs, desperately, to be *seen*, but she's not Linh, she's not Hoàng, she's not important enough to the country except as a bargaining chip. "We love each other, and that's all that should matter."

Mother's voice is hard. "Not when you're a princess of Bình Hải."

Thanh didn't want the conversation to go there—didn't want to have to say the words she now says—but there are no options left. "You said you wanted Bình Hải protected, no matter what it cost. You said I needed to understand that."

"I did." Mother's voice is faintly puzzled. "I don't see—"

"You don't?" Thanh's hand shows the board: Mother's scattered pieces, her own disarrayed army. She moves her general to face Mother's general across the board—a forbidden move, slowly and deliberately made to see the way Mother winces. "We're fighting each other, and in the end the board is clear for them to win." She moves her general away from the board entirely, sliding it off to join the other pieces Mother took. "But if I become Eldris's consort, they'll leave Bình Hải."

"Why would they?"

"Because you'll no longer be a challenge to them," Thanh says. "You sent me to Yosolis because you wanted me to know how they thought. Well, I can tell you how Eldris thinks. And Eldris's opinion is going to be the one that matters."

"The one that matters."

"She'll be queen," Thanh says, slowly, simply.

"And so will you." Mother's voice is sharp. "I didn't think you craved power quite that much."

How—how does she even begin to voice this? That it's not about power, that it's not about how many people whose lives she can bend to her will, but simply about being in control of her own life? She can't voice this, not in a way that Mother would understand. So instead she says, keeping her hands carefully away from the chess pieces, "I've said yes, and I won't take it back."

Mother's voice is speculative. "I could confine you to your rooms. Or disown you."

Thanh keeps her voice level, even, her eyes stubbornly on the scattering of pieces on the board. "You're free to do as you wish." She doesn't move, doesn't say anything else. She doesn't have the words anymore.

Mother moves, in a swish of cloth. Thanh doesn't—she still stares at the board. "You'll just run away, won't you. Do as you please. You've always been so stubborn. So selfish."

"I'm not stubborn!" Thanh doesn't answer the other accusation—because how could she? It's not for Bình Hải or Mother or the negotiations, for all her protestations that it's the best path. No: it's merely because of the way Eldris looks at her—of the way she dissects situations and makes Thanh feel at the center of it all. She says, slowly and coldly, "I learnt enough in Yosolis." Lack of filial piety, and pleasure taken where she will—and power and the meaning of it—and what it means to expect the entire world to shift around her. "Exactly the lessons you sent me there for." She waits, with the ball of guilt and sick fear forming in her gut—the same ball she's been curling around all her life: the knowledge she's gone too far, too fast, that this time Mother will truly abandon her, the way she's abandoned so many others.

"Don't you dare use that tone with me." Mother's voice is low and angry, and then it smooths out, becomes the empress's voice again. "I see. I suppose it's not that dire, in the end. A betrothal ceremony here certainly would help Bình Hải regain some of the prestige it's lost with your behavior."

Her behavior. Negotiating in a panic, making herself vulnerable. The ball in Thanh's belly becomes a vise squeezing her innards. It's not her fault. She knows it's not her fault. It's Mother being angry again, never admitting to fault. But she loves Thanh, nevertheless. She wants the best for Bình Hải and for Thanh. "Mother."

Mother says, "I'll present it to the ministers and officials of the court. The best path forward for Bình Hải: a reinforcement of old alliances. And of course you'll be able to advocate for us once you're in Yosolis." The tone makes it clear it's not a request Thanh can refuse. A clink of ivory on wood; as Thanh looks up Mother reaches for her own general and sets it square in the center of the board, in the river—a large boundary between both sides of the board, an area where no piece is meant to go or stay.

She could say no. She could stand up and do this on her terms, but it took all the energy she had for this confrontation, and she's got so little left. "Yes, Mother."

Mother smiles, and it's like Pharanea's: sharp teeth the color of bleached bones. "Superb. Was there anything else, child?"

"No, nothing." Thanh bows to take her leave. The ball in her lower belly hasn't moved: as she touches her forehead to the floor, she feels it climb up, a nauseous feeling of not knowing whether she's got what she came for.

The memory of Mother's smile follows her out of the room and into the corridors—a disquiet that refuses to go away.

~

"So?" Eldris asks. "How did it go?"

They're walking hand in hand in the gardens, by the pond. Frogs hop on lotus pads, and lanterns sway in the breeze. Eldris is holding Thanh's hand: she didn't try to ask anything for the first few minutes, just patiently waited for Thanh to speak. But of course, patience only goes so far—especially for Eldris.

Thanh says, finally, "I don't know. But she'll announce it to the council. And she'll hold a formal betrothal ceremony."

Eldris's face changes—it's like it's flooded with light. "That sounds like it went more than well."

Thanh still remembers the ball of guilt—the touch of the chess pieces on her hand, the way it all welled up in her until she wasn't sure if she was going to hold herself together. "I'm sure," she says. It's hard to muster enthusiasm.

Eldris stops. "Thanh. You did it. That's all that matters." And she kisses her, slowly and carefully—and Thanh feels herself bloom, feels seen and valued. "Think of the future. *Our* future."

It's blank—something barely seen, barely imagined, terrifying in its formlessness. "I don't know what it would look like."

Eldris holds out her hand to Thanh, and in her pale palm is a ring: a silver circle with a sapphire the sharp, pale color of the winter sky and two smaller diamonds on either side, a piece of Yosolis's cold climes offered to her. "Here. This is for you. A small token."

An engagement ring.

Thanh picks it up, feeling the weight and coldness of it. She slips it on, feels it encircle her finger, the cold spreading to her skin. Eldris is watching her with a fond smile, but something in the intensity of her gaze makes Thanh queasy.

"Us," Eldris says. "That's what it will look like. Us, together. Walking the Leuthe park in the morning—taking petitions in the afternoon—racing each other in the snow. Like it was, those months when we were together."

Thanh thinks of snow and winter, of boats and long journeys—of Eldris, holding her, always there to steady her. The lanterns sway overhead—and the crisp memory of snow becomes tinged with ashes—and abruptly she's holding Giang's hand and running in the midst of corridors that are aflame, and everything is fire, everything is smoke, and she'll die here choking to death, breathing in the air of a country that's not hers, but no country is hers anymore . . .

"Thanh? Thanh? My love!"

It's Eldris, shaking her. Her blue eyes are wide with worry. "Are you all right?"

Thanh shivers. "I remembered the fire."

"Ah." A silence, from Eldris. "Some things always burn bright, don't they?"

Not for her. Of course never for her. But for her and for Giang . . .

Giang.

She completely forgot about Giang.

Giang, whom she lied to. Who deserves better than what Thanh has done to her. "Eldris," she says, slowly and urgently. "I need to go. There's something I need to sort out."

For a moment she sees storm clouds gather on Eldris's face—and braces herself for an explosion, for the temper

Eldris has always lost so easily—and then Eldris visibly forces herself to relax. "Something?"

"Negotiations," Thanh says, curtly.

"Surely these aren't needed anymore?" Eldris shakes her head, fondly. "But of course. I wouldn't want to get in the way of your responsibilities. Go. I'll see you tonight?"

"Of course." Thanh runs her hand on Eldris's face, feeling in the cool smoothness of her—her rock amidst the upheavals of her life. "Always, my love."

Eldris smiles, and kisses her back—and everything contracts, and desire slowly arches its way up her back, as Eldris's tongue finds her—and then she withdraws, and Thanh stands up, gasping for breath, arms reaching for a princess who's no longer there "Till tonight," Eldris says.

Thanh starts walking back—and then running. Giang. She has to tell Giang before the betrothal ceremony—before it becomes palace gossip even a very unaware fire elemental cannot ignore. She can't find any lanterns on her way—no fire, no embers, nothing she can use to call on Giang.

"Going somewhere?" Captain Pharanea's voice, silky and threatening.

No.

"Get out of my way," Thanh says, curtly. She shouldn't stop, but Pharanea has moved to block the pillared passage into the courtyard leading to the Inner Quarters.

"I think not." Pharanea's smile is predatory. "We had an agreement. You can hardly keep it if you insist on kissing and fondling each other in public places." She spits the words like they're poison, all subtlety gone. "I should have known you wouldn't be able to behave."

Something twists in Thanh's belly: fear, the knowledge that Pharanea doesn't really want to keep their agreement. She thinks Thanh is a savage, not worth respecting. "I had my fill of etiquette teachers," she says, speaking through a mouth that feels filled with cotton.

"Light wasted on the blind." Pharanea snorts. "On the weak."

She sounds like Mother—and something primal stirs in Thanh, a spike of fear, a sickness clenching her belly, the lack of options—and then she remembers that nothing Pharanea does can touch her anymore. She draws herself to her full height. "I told Mother."

Pharanea's face twists in pure hatred. "You did what?"

Thanh takes a step back—and then Eldris is there, sword unsheathed, standing between them both like the answer to a prayer Thanh didn't even have to utter.

"Your Highness." Pharanea's voice is shaking. Light plays on the drawn blade, shivers and breaks into a thousand reflections. "She's not worth it."

Eldris's entire stance hardens. "Are you talking about my fiancée?"

Pharanea's face goes white. "Your Highness." Her mouth works, stops. She's about to tell Eldris—to her face—that she can't possibly make that choice.

Eldris's smile is razor-sharp. "Go on. Say it." She holds the blade, lightly.

Pharanea doesn't move. She's weighing options: trying to see if Eldris would dare to cut her down, wondering if she ought to remind Eldris of the consequences if she dies—of her many titles, of her many allies at court. Finally she says, "I apologize if I offended you, Your Highness." And bows, low and abject.

Eldris doesn't move. Neither does the blade. "I'm not the one you offended." Her chin moves, towards Thanh.

"Your Highness!"

The blade moves—held to Pharanea's cheek, gently pressing down until a drop of blood pearls. Pharanea's face is the color of snow and ashes. "You—" She swallows, audibly.

"I would," Eldris says, and her voice is almost gentle. The sword moves—the blood on it dripping down to fall upon the earth.

At length, Pharanea says, "Your Highness," to Thanh. "My apologies. It won't happen again."

Thanh nods. She ought to say something. She ought to thank Eldris for standing up for her; she ought to be grateful. But all she feels is that same sick thing in her innards, and words scattering in her mind, and all she can see is blood on the blade. It seems so easy, so much less fraught, to remain silent.

Eldris withdraws the sword. She and Pharanea continue to look at each other. "Thanh?" Eldris says, with only the barest of looks at her. "You can leave. Pharanea and I will sort this out." She cleans the sword, and sheathes it. "Like civilized people." Her voice is amused and bitter all at once.

Thanh runs away, not looking back.

~

As Thanh runs, she feels Giang: in the lanterns overhead, in the wash of sunlight like bloodred fingers across the sky, in each and every gleam of light on lacquered pillars.

Everything that burns in the palace calls to me, big sis. And you're upset.

She feels Giang's hand in hers, remembers fire and smoke—and sees, again and again, the glint on Eldris's blade, the drops of blood dripping to the floor.

Pharanea and I will sort this out. Like civilized people.

When she gets, out of breath, to her rooms, she finds Giang sitting on the bed, waiting for her. "Big sis." She doesn't ask what's wrong, or why, or how, but simply holds Thanh's hand, waiting. Her touch is as warm as fire.

"You're afraid," Giang says, slowly and carefully. "Of me?"

Thanh looks up. Giang's human face is a faint outline, and the stripes of the tiger's carving waver in and out of existence on her skin. She's the fire—the one that's haunted her nightmares for so long, the one that she's feared for so long. Except . . . except it's not Giang she's scared of, and she dares not voice the other, darker thought—dares not give a name to other nightmares. "No," Thanh says.

Giang doesn't speak, for a while. "Something happened."

Thanh closes her eyes. "Yes." And, remembering what she wanted to do before Pharanea stopped her. "I lied to you."

"Lied?" Giang cocks her head. "I don't understand. Thanh, that's not—"

"I know." Thanh shakes her head. "Please. Hear me out. Please."

Giang moves away, settling on her haunches.

"The woman who came to my rooms," Thanh said. "She wanted me to stop seeing Princess Eldris."

Giang goes very still. "Seeing."

You matter.

"We—" Thanh swallows. There's no easy way to say this, to make it palatable. "We're betrothed. We're going to get married." She stubbornly avoids looking at the sapphire ring on her finger, focusing instead on Giang's face, on Giang's voice.

"I know what a betrothal is. I'm not totally ignorant." Giang's voice is bitter.

She *is* upset. It is absurd. Fire elementals can't possibly *care* about humans. Can't possibly—

Thanh can't bring herself to say the words.

Giang isn't speaking. She's staring at her hands. Silence spreads, heavy and uncomfortable, much like Thanh's mother not speaking after Thanh has disappointed her one too many times. Thanh says something, to paper over her panicked sense of letting everyone else in her life down. "You're worried about where you'll go if I leave. We can talk about this."

Giang startles. Her eyes, when she looks at Thanh, are the red of fire: the fire elemental who'll scorch the earth. But when she speaks, it's not the anger Thanh is expecting. "I'm not going back to Yosolis, but I don't have to be here, you know"—and her voice becomes barbed and edged and it's almost a relief because it's something familiar—"I could just leave. Burn some trees in the jungle, or go in villages' communal halls. They have nice, warm fires."

"You're not happy," Thanh says. It's her fault. It's everything she's done and every lie she's told. How did she possibly expect things to turn otherwise?

"Why wouldn't I be?" Giang laughs. She stretches, slow and careful. "Big sis, it's your life. You go through it the way you want. You—" She stops then, starts again, "Your life doesn't come with an obligation to make mine work."

Something stretches thin in Thanh's chest, constricting her breath. She tries to speak, but nothing comes out.

Giang is still staring at her—alien and distant, limned in the warmth of the flames. Any moment now she'll turn into the being of Thanh's nightmares—the fire that engulfed the palace, that still haunts her. She'll speak and Thanh will only hear the roar of the flames. But Giang's next words are simply, "I'm sorry. I shouldn't have said that. It was hurtful."

They're impossible words. They ring, over and over, in Thanh's mind, an endless string of incoherent syllables. She can't be spoken to like this. She doesn't *deserve* to be spoken to like this. "Please don't say that."

"Why not?"

"*Please,*" Thanh says. Because Giang should be angry. Because Giang should be blaming her. Because—because anger is easier, and compassion hurts so much. And, because she knows no other way, she says, "I don't know why you care so much about hurt. It's not like you'd know what it means."

Giang stares at her for a while, with those same wide, gleaming eyes. Something catches in Thanh's chest: a heartbeat, skipped; a warm breath like a kiss, swallowed and treasured. She doesn't deserve that. She never deserved that. "You know why," Giang says. A shake of her head that limns it in flames. "I told you."

You matter.

"No," Thanh says. "No." That's not possible. That's the stuff of legends and fairy tales, of the founding of kingdoms. Not of now, in this beleaguered kingdom where every choice feels it's leading to ever smaller places.

"Of course it is." Giang sounds as though she's going to say something else, stops with a visible effort. "Are you going to tell me what I feel?"

"You don't know what you're saying."

"That's not true." And she's looking at Thanh with such bright, naked hunger that Thanh sees what's been staring her in the face.

"No," she says. "You can't—"

But she can, can't she? She understands fear and anger and atonement and the desire to make herself smaller to do less harm. Why would she not understand other feelings, too?

"I care about you. I—you're right: I don't know what it is; I don't know what it means." She takes a small, shaking breath. "I've never felt this before."

"Giang—"

"You do what you want with this. It's not for me to tell you how to receive it. But—" Another shaking breath that limns the room in fire. "But I have to say it, big sis. *She would have let you burn.*"

She doesn't need to say Eldris's name. Her words are as sharp as a knife stab, and guilt and anger well up in Thanh. *How dare she?* "We weren't together at the time."

Giang says, simply, "When the palace was burning, she left without once thinking of you."

"They all did," Thanh says.

"Yes." Giang flicks her fingers, spreading something that looks like ashes over the bed. "You say Eldris wouldn't have done this if she'd been in love with you. What I'm asking is: If love is what it takes to make her remember a girl in the midst of a fire, then how much can you trust her? How much can you trust that love?"

Blood on a sword. Pharanea's pale face. Eldris's voice when she spoke of the other countries they'd conquer. "That's nonsense."

Giang says nothing, merely holds her ground and stares at Thanh. *How dare she? How dare she?*

"You're a fire elemental. You don't know. You can't know any of those things. You hurt people. You burnt the palace. You killed so many. What can you know about love, Giang?"

Giang's face is pale, her breath faster and faster, contracting the light around the room as if it were flames, flickering in the shadow of a burning building. "Big sis."

"Shut up. I don't want to hear it. I don't want to hear any of it. You don't know what you're talking about. You can't possibly know. Just leave me alone!" And Thanh gets up and paces the room—and when she looks again Giang is gone, and there are only ashes like white snow on the bed, and the echo of Giang's voice in the room, already fading.

"As you wish."

~

Alone in her room, Thanh paces up and down, trying to banish the memory of fire. "Giang?" she calls. "Li'l sis?"

There's no answer. "Li'l sis!"

In the antechamber, the handmaidens are playing a game of mạt chược, and laughing every time one of them puts a particularly auspicious combination down. Thanh sits down on the bed, breathing hard. Nibbles a bun from the tray by the bedside, finding it tastes like ashes—the same ashes Giang spread on her bed, before she left. All the lanterns in the room have gone out: not even warm embers left in them. She's gone—to some other fire, as she said, some other refuge. Always plenty to burn.

I care.

What has she done?

She gets up again. The room is small and stifling and she cannot seem to banish Giang's eyes from her thoughts. She kneels, instead, before her clothes chests, pulling out the one for the dry season and lifting out silk clothes from within. She might as well pack for Yosolis. It will keep her mind on the important things. On what she's chosen for herself.

Outside, the mạt chược game has fallen silent. Thanh unfolds dress after dress, staring at the beautiful embroidery—are these golden birds worth taking back to Yosolis, or will they make her seem like more of a foreigner? She'll have to look at the jewelry, too.

A murmur of voices from the antechamber. Thanh barely looks up—but then she hears Eldris's voice, sharp and cutting.

The door slams open. It's Eldris, face flushed. Thanh gets up, holding a dress in front of her. "My love—"

"Where is she?" Eldris asks.

Pharanea? But surely Eldris would know... "I don't understand—"

"Don't lie to me." Eldris's voice is sharp. "Your hand-maidens talked. You have someone else in your bed-room. Where is she?"

Giang. Thanh's heart chills. She's done nothing improper with Giang, nothing at all, but she can't help the pang of guilt that surges through her. "Eldris, I swear it's nothing—"

Eldris pushes past Thanh, pulls clothes from the dry season chest, and throws them on the bed. "Where is she, Thanh?"

Thanh still holds the dress, a flimsy shield between them. "She's not here now." And then realizes what she's said.

Eldris's gaze turns to stone. "But she was here. Wasn't she?" And, when Thanh doesn't move: "Answer me!"

"I don't sleep with her," Thanh says.

"I don't care!" Eldris's face is contorted into what might be grief, or anger. "You hid her, Thanh. I embarrassed myself in front of Pharanea for you—and now I discover you've been running so fast because you wanted to get back to someone I've never met? That you've been holding out on me. What did you think you were doing?"

"Eldris," Thanh says—and Eldris covers the space between them, and tears the dress away from her, and Thanh feels as though she's been stripped naked. "I love you. Please don't—"

"You said yes. You're my bride," Eldris says. "I didn't come all this way to be lied to, Thanh."

She raises her hand again, and with icy clarity, Thanh sees it—that she's going to strike, to send Thanh tumbling to the bed. And then ... her mind balks, but she knows all the outcomes, knows that none of them are good for her. Mother's soldiers will come here, of course, but by the time they arrive it'll be too late for her.

Mother's words in her memory, each of them precise and clipped: *She's here to take what she wants.*

And Giang's voice, small and thin: *How much can you trust that love?*

Thanh catches Eldris's hand in hers—feels the shock of it traveling up her wrist and arm; strains to remain standing. And then she twists, and as Eldris is thrown off-balance she runs for the door.

The antechamber is deserted, the handmaidens gone, and their mạt chược tiles scattered on the floor. They're carved ivory: any of them can send her face-first on the floor, a fall that'll cost her dearly. Thanh dances around them, breath in her throat: behind her she can hear Eldris throwing open the door, can hear the sound of the sword's scabbard, that slow steady beating against Eldris's legs. She sidesteps, again and again, starts feeling her foot slipping—shakes it, panicked, until her smooth-soled shoes are gone and it's just her bare feet, and she's past the antechamber, and at the top of a short flight of steps leading down to a courtyard. Over her is the roof, with the longevity tiles, and lanterns swinging in the breeze.

Eldris's hand on her shoulder, unwavering. "Don't

leave." Thanh struggles, but her grip is too strong, and she's pulling her in. "Let's talk."

"I don't have anything else to say," Thanh says, but Eldris's grip doesn't waver.

"Apologies would be appropriate." Eldris's voice is flat now, the same tone she had in the audience chamber at the very beginning. It's not going to stop at talking. It'll be groveling and humiliation, if it ends there at all. Thanh's eyes, wildly searching, find the lanterns above her, the gleam of embers there.

"Li'l sis!" She calls—and again and again, as Eldris pulls at her. "Li'l sis, please. I'm sorry. Please." *Please please please.* She can't throw off Eldris's grip: it's hard enough to bruise.

"She's not here," Eldris says, slowly, viciously.

Thanh, the fire whispers in the courtyard. *Big sis.* The embers flare in the lanterns. Fire flickers and grows—spins into the air, lands at the foot of the stairs, and takes the shape of a woman.

Giang.

She pulls herself upwards, staring at Eldris—staring at Thanh, with wide, luminous eyes. "Let her go," she says.

Eldris has frozen. Thanh tries to free herself, but the grip on her hasn't wavered.

"What sorcery is this?" Eldris says.

Giang stares levelly back at her. She doesn't move, but

she seems to grow larger and taller, her hands stretching into claws, her eyes catching fire, her skin golden and striped. Light spreads beneath her skin, as if it was just a thin, papery shell over ever-burning flames.

"Let her go," Giang says, again, and the light spreads—and when it reaches the columns, they catch fire.

It's a faint, translucent shadow—the ghost of flames, something that doesn't seem to touch the wood—and yet Thanh smells smoke, and charring, and the promise of more: of rooms ablaze and corridors aflame. Behind her, Eldris stands frozen. It's her chance: there will never be a better one. Thanh jabs behind her with her elbow, straight into Eldris's ribs—and as Eldris gasps, she frees herself and stumbles blindly down the steps, towards the center of the courtyard. Comes to stand away from them both, rubbing at her shoulder where she still feels the shock of Eldris's grip—the way it's slowly segueing into a dull, throbbing pain.

Eldris raised her hand. She threw clothes on the bed. She grabbed Thanh.

She—words spin and falter and fail Thanh utterly.

On the steps, Giang is staring at Eldris. Eldris looks from her to Thanh—and then says, very quietly, "I see. You could have had so much."

A gilded cage. A ring of thorns, gnawing her to the

bone. Thanh forces herself to stand still, when everything in her screams of flight. She says—because darkness needs to be faced, needs to be denied—"You would have given me so much, in exchange for me giving up everything."

"Don't be so melodramatic."

But she knows she's not. She knows that the drama maker is the one who rifled through clothes and would have pushed Thanh to the bed.

"No," Thanh says, simply.

Eldris gazes back at her. And then, slowly and deliberately, turns and walks away without a backward glance, alongside the covered corridors of pillars leading outside Thanh's quarters, and back into the gardens. Abandoning Thanh—a pawn that's served her purpose, that no longer deserves anything. It shouldn't hurt so much. It shouldn't feel like someone is ripping her heart out. "Eldris—" Thanh bites back on a cry of pure anguish.

But it's Giang's voice that is louder. "You don't walk away," she says. "You don't get to take what you want, what you think you're due simply because no one has ever refused you." And she moves, then—the light of the fire extending ahead of her, towards Eldris. Eldris starts running alongside the corridor, one hand on the hilt of her sword, and Giang follows her. As she does every pillar on either side of the corridor goes up like kindling, little flames spreading to the carvings and the lanterns in the rafters, and the stones under her becoming opalescent as if with trapped light.

No no no.

It smells of fire and smoke, and the steps Thanh tumbled down are covered in ghostly flames, the stone luminous and orange. Thanh moves towards them, feels the heat underfoot; smells fire and smoke, and hears the crackle of burning wood. She's alone again, powerless and forgotten. She's running through the corridors of the palace in Yosolis and finding only burning rooms and courtyards full of ashes and choking smoke until it seems to her she's forgotten what it means to freely breathe. Eldris and the others are already safely outside, where the real princesses are, where the people who matter got evacuated—she doesn't matter; she's never mattered.

She—

She remembers Giang's hand in hers, remembers running through corridors. Remembers that, in the midst of bleak despair, she found the way out for both of them.

That's what matters.

She's not in Yosolis anymore, and if she doesn't stop Giang there will be nothing left of her home.

Worse, there will be nothing left of Giang; of the girl who looked at Thanh with wide eyes; the one Thanh befriended, the one who held her hand and whose touch made Thanh's breath catch. The one who—

The one whom Thanh cares for, just as Giang cares for her.

She can't let Giang lose herself here.

Thanh closes her eyes; breathes in, slowly and deliberately, feeling the acrid taste of smoke in her lungs. Then she starts running.

They haven't gone far: only to the next courtyard, one with a pond and pavilion—the pond's water has evaporated, the lotus flowers are ablaze, and the pavilion is falling to charred pieces. In its ruins, Eldris stands, disheveled and wild, holding her sword against Giang with a manic gleam in her eyes. Giang is now something else—a creature of claws and fire, awaiting a chance to devour it all. The flames gather around her like a court of attendants, and in the center is barely a hint of the girl in Thanh's bedroom, the one who was finding buns odd. There's just a dark shadow, with yellow eyes the color of amber, elongated pupils—with a stretched mouth full of fangs, and claws gleaming sharper than any human steel.

This. This is who burnt the palace in Yosolis.

"Giang. Li'l sis. Please."

Giang turns, a fraction. Faces Thanh, her head cocking curiously, a tiger unsure of its prey.

"It's me," Thanh says. Giang isn't recognizing her. She'll swallow her whole, as casually as she's burnt everything—as she'd have burnt Eldris. Thanh says, with a confidence she doesn't feel—heart beating frantically in her throat—"Remember."

A shrug, from Giang.

"Li'l sis. Giang. You—you said everything you touched caught fire. You said you didn't know what you'd done. You said you hadn't meant to burn the palace."

A pause. The claws stretch, lazily, towards her. "If you do this, it'll be deliberate." *Ancestors, please watch over me. Please please please.* "You'll be responsible for it. All of it."

Giang says, in a voice that's the crackle of flames, "She would have killed you. Or worse."

Thanh stares at Eldris—at the sword, at the face that looks like a stranger's. "Yes," she says, and the word tastes bitter on her tongue. Because that's who Eldris is, and it hurts to admit it. "But she's not worth it." That hurts, too.

"She'll come back," Giang says. "To conquer you. To reduce you to a different sort of ashes."

She might. She might not. "Yes," Thanh says. "But that's not how you solve it. Li'l sis, please. You said you cared. You said I mattered. You said you didn't want to hurt me. This will hurt. This is my home you're burning."

A pause. An eternity while the courtyard burns around her—while she digs her nails into her hands to not run away, to not find fresh air and coolness and everything that's not fire.

Giang says, finally, "I want you safe."

Thanh swallows back bitter tears. "There's nothing that keeps me safe. Not the way you or she want." Not the way Eldris wants. Because that safety is a cage. It's Thanh held in amber, forever shielded by someone else's will.

Giang looks at her. The darkness at the heart of the fire is dwindling, and when she speaks again it's with the voice of the girl. "I'm not her."

"I know," Thanh says. She's meant to keep her voice low and quiet, but it slips out all the same, as if she'd been holding it in her the entire time and running finally dislodged it. "I care for you."

Giang's voice is shaking. "Big sis."

Thanh says it again, because it's the only thing left in her. "I care for you. I—stay with me, Giang, please. Will you stay with me?"

Giang smiles, and it's wide and careless once more. "Of course I'll always stay with you." She moves—and the flames become transparent again, the stones dark and solid. "Go," she says, to Eldris.

Eldris doesn't need to be told twice. She sheathes her sword, and walks—and then runs, getting out of sight in less time than it takes the flames at the pavilion to subside.

Thanh and Giang stare at each other. Giang's corona of flame is still around her, and behind her the corridor is still burning, with shouts from the palace's fire brigade to bring water. In a moment, there will be people—attendants, scholars, counsellors—an irate, desolate Mother who will need to be reassured, or placated, or both. In a moment the world will intrude again on the reality of it all.

In a moment.

Thanh covers the distance that separates them both. She reaches out, holding both of Giang's hands in hers—feeling only a faint warmth, a memory of what once terrified her. Her shoulder still aches where Eldris grabbed her, and her heart feels overlarge in her chest. "I'm sorry," she says. "I shouldn't have—"

Giang raises a hand, slowly and tentatively. And when Thanh doesn't move away, she rests two fingers on Thanh's lips, and Thanh can feel the quivering pulse in these. "It's all right, big sis," Giang says. "It's all right."

But it's not.

～

Mother is not happy. She summons priests and advisers, and Thanh says deliberately confused things about fire and assault and Eldris. Giang has left, after Thanh forcefully insisted—it's bad enough without adding a loose fire elemental in the mix.

When Thanh is done, Mother stares at her for a while—weighing her, trying to sort out truth from lies. Thanh feels her shoulder, again and again. Will the memory of Eldris's touch ever go away?

At length, Mother's lips thin into a colorless slit. "You will let me handle this," she says to Thanh.

"Mother—"

"You've done enough damage." And she turns away, to Long—Thanh dismissed as if she were a child. "Search the palace. There's a sorcerer or a magician here. An Ephterian, likely."

Long grimaces. "And if we find them?"

Thanh cannot see Mother's face. But she hears the grimness in her tone. "Ask them to leave. You know as well as I do that there's nothing more we can do."

Extraterritoriality. Of course, with the betrothal gone, they'll have no choice but to accept Ephterian terms.

Mother glares at Eldris's sapphire ring, which is still on Thanh's finger. "Give me the ring," Mother says to Thanh. She holds out her hand.

Thanh closes her hand, turning the ring inward so the stone is hidden in her palm. It's not that she wants it—but the order grates. Mother stares at her for a while. "You're in shock. Go back to your room. We'll see each other in the morning."

Guards escort Thanh to her room, and then they're

all gone, and there's just her—and the weight of the ring in her hand, and the fading hurt on her shoulder from where Eldris grabbed her—the pain is gone, but it still feels like Eldris has taken a piece of her flesh with her.

"Big sis." It's Giang, sitting on the bed, with a frown on her face. "I'm sorry. I shouldn't have—"

In her face is only anguish. Of course. She almost burnt down the palace. She almost did what she'd sworn never to do. Thanh closes her hand on the sapphire again, and draws Giang into her embrace, feeling the warmth of her against her body, repeating Giang's words at her. "Ssshhh. It's all right." And does it matter that it's not, if it gets them through the night?

A short, bitter laugh from Giang. "Will it be?"

There's nothing that keeps me safe.

Nothing that keeps her unharmed or out of danger's way. But—

But.

Thanh thinks of Eldris; thinks of Mother; thinks of letters, and of the shape of politics around her, of what the future can hold. "It just might, if we put down our tiles just the right way."

～

Thanh sits bolt upright by Mother's side in the throne room, watching the Ephterians file in.

They walk slowly with their heads held high: Pharanea with the mark of Eldris's sword on her cheek, flanked by the other two, and behind her Eldris.

Her face is pale, and she will not meet Thanh's gaze. Her sword taps against her legs as she walks, and if Thanh closes her eyes she'll smell fire and blood, and feel phantom pain on her shoulder.

She keeps her eyes open. Beside her, Mother says, simply, "Remember: You will let me handle this. Do not speak unless I ask you to."

The Ephterians bow, silently, to Mother. There is tea on the table—fresh and green—and a host of officials in the room, waiting with heads bowed for the outcome of this meeting. "Sit down," Mother says. "We need to talk about apologies."

She's told Thanh off already, but of course she cannot let this provocation happen in her own court. Thanh can see all the ways this is going to go, the slow, careful dance that will lead to them bowing to Ephteria once again, to be broken once again.

It's the price she has to pay for standing up. For almost killing Eldris and burning down half the palace. It makes sense—like everything Mother has ever done.

She can imagine Giang, and what Giang would say to

that: *Just because it makes sense doesn't mean it needs to happen that way.*

"Li'l sis," she whispers, and the lanterns waver in the breeze—and Giang is standing at the back of the court, a ghostly shape that is gaining color and form, as if an artist were passing successive washes of paint over her. She looks straight at Thanh with bright, luminous eyes.

Thanh stands up. She slides off the ring Eldris gave her, drops it on the dais. It clatters with a sound like a bell's call. She says, simply, "We don't want apologies. Nor will we tender any."

Mother, shocked and angry, gestures towards the guards, but before she can finish Giang stretches in the doorway of the throne room and the fire in the lanterns flares sharply up with a whooshing noise like flames, drawing her gaze to them—and in that moment of frozen shock Thanh speaks up. "I've written to Ngân Kỳ. You'll find that threatening the life of an imperial princess who is also a betrothed bride, and causing a wing of the palace to be destroyed, is an act beyond the boundaries of what they'll allow from uncouth foreigners."

Eldris says, sharply, "They owe us."

"Yes," Thanh says. "So do we. You'll also find that it's much harder to parcel us out when we jointly say no."

Mother stares at Thanh. She opens her mouth, and her gaze finds that of Adviser Long, who simply shakes his head. Thanh can feel the beads of the abacus in Mother's mind, clacking against each other as they slide into place—as she finishes the political calculus Thanh has started for her. "Continue," she says to Thanh, as smoothly and gracefully as if this were all planned.

"I've offered them an alliance," Thanh says. "I don't think they'll refuse it."

They won't. The imperial palace is sacred; so is the life of a bride.

"You cannot—" Pharanea starts.

"In my own palace?" Mother's voice is sweet the way of poisoned honey.

Eldris's gaze moves from Mother to Thanh. "You," she says, her eyes narrowing, and her hand goes to the hilt of her sword. She's going to cut Thanh down—too fast for anyone in the room to do anything about this. She—

No, she's not. She's trying to make Thanh afraid, and two can play at that game. "Eldris," Thanh says, sharply. "Look behind you."

Eldris turns. Giang is walking between the assembled officials—not walking so much as running in front of guards trying to intercept her. Fire flickers on her hand, on the stripes on her face. She's looking straight at Eldris, and smiling, showing the fangs in her mouth—and Eldris takes a step back, pale and shaken—and another and another until she's at the rightmost hand of the dais.

Mother lifts a hand, and the guards stop. So does Giang, but she doesn't look away from Eldris.

Thanh speaks, in the silence. "I think it's time you left."

"Your Highness?" Pharanea asks.

"You heard her," Eldris snaps. "Let's go."

She doesn't look at Thanh as she leaves, but Thanh looks at her. She watches her walk away, watches the way the sword swings—watches her legs and the sweep of her shoulders—and thinks of a pavilion, and of lips on hers, and of trust and of everything they once had. It takes all she has to stand still, to not run after her and beg Eldris to take her back—or to scream at her for the harsh words, for the violence. She doesn't know, not anymore, but she feels the moment Eldris leaves the throne room; feels the way the air becomes lighter in her lungs, the way muscles clenched in fear slowly relax.

"Big sis." Giang is at her side, and Thanh turns to her, the noise of the court fading away.

"You'll have to introduce me to your . . . friend." Mother's voice is sharp, but not unkind.

Thanh reaches out, finds Giang's hand. "This is Giang, Mother. If you'll excuse us—"

She half-expects Mother or an official to stop them as they walk out of the throne room. She keeps tensing, waiting for it—but there's nothing, and then she and Giang are standing on the platform, looking down on the immense courtyard with the dragon and pearl emblem of Bình Hải spread on the pavement below them.

"Thank you for your help," Thanh says.

Giang shrugs. "That was nothing. You did most of it, you know."

"*We* did it," Thanh says. They're gone. The Ephterians are gone. What follows will be neither easy nor pleasant, but there is a way forward that wasn't there before.

They stare at each other in awkward silence.

Giang is the one to break it. "What now?"

"I don't know," Thanh says. "That thing you feel for me—"

Giang says, simply, "Love."

"Love," Thanh says. The word feels too raw, too fragile—too soiled by what Eldris has done. "I don't know, li'l sis. Not yet. I feel . . . a connection between us. A start." A seed in a garden; and given enough time and healing, what flower might it blossom into?

"A connection. It's all right," Giang says. "I can wait for you to figure it out."

"For *us* to figure it out."

"Li'l sis. Of course. For us." Giang moves towards Thanh, slowly, carefully—they kiss and it's tentative and Thanh feels as though she's breaking inside, undone by warmth. "I can stop—" Giang says.

"Don't you dare," Thanh says, and kisses her

again—and holds her close until the warmth of fire makes the memory of Eldris shrivel and contract into harmlessness. Giang's hands rest on her shoulders, and Thanh's hands wrap around Giang's waist, feeling the curve of her spine beneath the striped skin, the fast and steady beating of Giang's heart.

There will be explanations, introductions; arguments with Mother and with Adviser Long and the rest of the court. There will be a tomorrow and it will hold negotiations and boundaries; and the shape of Thanh's place in the court, irrevocably changed after what they've done—and the shape of Giang's place, because she, too, has changed. There will be so much to do and so much to untangle.

But for now, there is just the two of them, and the warmth that binds them both together—and the future that is theirs to shape.

Acknowledgments

With thanks to Tade Thompson, Kate Elliott, Vida Cruz, Fran Wilde, and Stephanie Burgis, and to Hara Trân for checking all the Vietnamese names in this. And to my ink posse and all my snarky, supportive friends who love hot steamed buns.

About the Author

Lou Abercrombie

ALIETTE DE BODARD lives and works in Paris. She has won three Nebula Awards, a Locus Award, a British Fantasy Award, and four British Science Fiction Association Awards, and was a double Hugo finalist for 2019 (Best Series and Best Novella). Most recently she published *The House of Sundering Flames,* the conclusion to her Dominion of the Fallen trilogy, set in a turn-of-the-century Paris devastated by a magical war, which also comprises *The House of Shattered Wings* and *The House of Binding Thorns.* Her short story collection, *Of Wars, and Memories, and Starlight,* is out from Subterranean Press.

TOR · COM

Science fiction. Fantasy. The universe.

And related subjects.

*

More than just a publisher's website, *Tor.com*
is a venue for **original fiction, comics,** and
discussion of the entire field of SF and fantasy,
in all media and from all sources. Visit our site
today—and join the conversation yourself.